MISSION: NEW BABY

For Emily and Allison—
the best big and little sisters ever!
—S.H.

For calvin
—M.L.

Text copyright © 2015 by Susan Hood
Cover art and interior illustrations copyright © 2015 by Mary Lundquist

Visit us on the Web! randomhousekids.com

Educators and librarians, for a variety of teaching tools, visit us at RHTeachersLibrarians.com

Library of Congress Cataloging-in-Publication Data
Hood, Susan.
Mission: new baby / by Susan Hood ; illustrated by Mary Lundquist. — First edition.
  pages cm.
Summary: "A secret agent's guide to welcoming a new sibling." —Provided by publisher.
ISBN 978-0-385-37672-3 (trade) — ISBN 978-0-375-97324-6 (lib. bdg.) — ISBN 978-0-375-98215-6 (ebook)
[1. Babies—Fiction. 2. Brothers and sisters—Fiction.] I. Lundquist, Mary, illustrator. II. Title.
PZ7.H763315Mi 2013 [E]—dc23 2013009061

Book design by John Sazaklis

MANUFACTURED IN CHINA
10 9 8 7 6 5 4 3 2 1
First Edition

MISSION:
NEW BABY

WRITTEN BY
SUSAN HOOD

ILLUSTRATED BY
MARY LUNDQUIST

TOP-SECRET INFO FOR BIG BROTHERS & SISTERS

Random House 🏠 New York

CONGRATULATIONS!

Headquarters is about to get a brand-new recruit. Since you're the BIG BROTHER or SISTER, your MISSION is to train the NEW kid on the team. It's a BIG job. Are you ready?

START HERE.

1. ATTEND BRIEFING.

#2. TEST GADGETS AND GEAR.

AND INTRODUCE
ASSOCIATES.

#5. SHOW CREDENTIALS.

#6. BEGIN INSTRUCTION.

#8. SET UP COMMUNICATION SYSTEMS.

#9. SHARE INTELLIGENCE.

#10.
LEAD PHYSICAL TRAINING AND PROVIDE BACKUP.

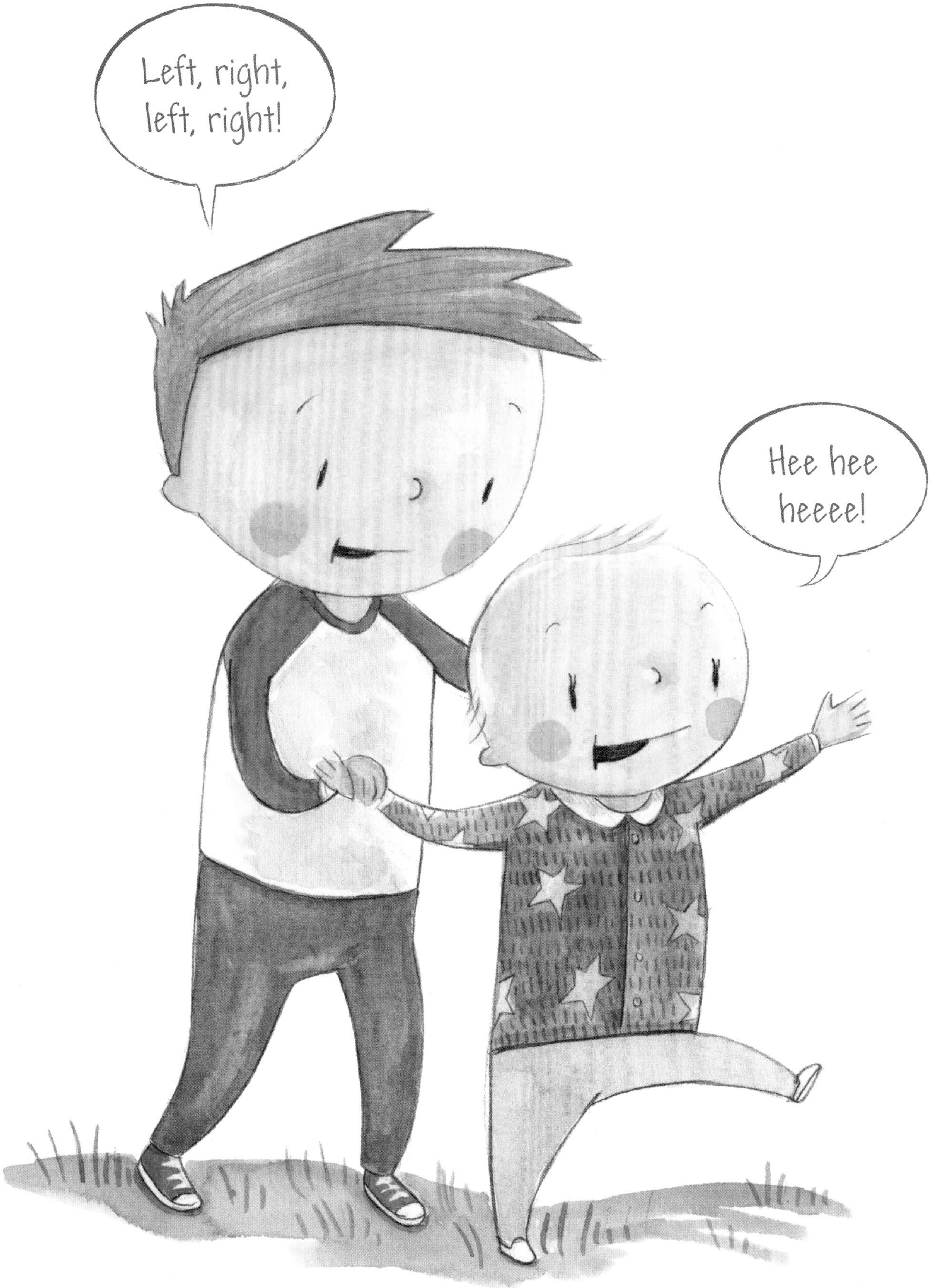
Left, right,
left, right!
Hee hee
heeee!

#11. BLEND IN.

#12.
COMPLETE
COVERT OPERATION.

#13. REPORT INCOMING MISSILES.

#14.
TEST
DISGUISES.

They'll never guess your identity now!

#15.
GO UNDERCOVER.

#16.
HUSH
SLEEPER
AGENTS.